Treading Water

Treading Water

Ed Mako

2003
Galde Press, Inc.
Lakeville, Minnesota, U.S.A.

Treading Water
© Copyright 2003 by Ed Mako
All rights reserved.
Printed in the United States of America
No part of this book may be used or reproduced in any manner whatsoever without written permission from the publishers except in the case of brief quotations embodied in critical articles and reviews.

First Edition
First Printing, 2003

Cover design by Andrew Wood

Galde Press, Inc.
PO Box 460
Lakeville, Minnesota 55044–0460

Contents

Acknowledgments   xi

Just People
   Boy in the Oak   3
   Ahab, Ahab, Why Dost Thou?   5
   Carol   7
   Hester   9
   She Is Eighty   11
   She   13
   Isabella   15
   What Now, Frank?   17
   Puzzle Pieces   19
   Piece Work   21
   Poker   23
   Julian of Norwich   27
   Mary   29
   A Prayer to Lady Wisdom   31
   The Good Man   33

Bits and Pieces Lightly Played
   Sun Dress   37
   Cherry Blossom   39

   Ifs and Hopes   41
   Kissed Me   41
   Little Boys and Little Girls   41

   Oh! Those Suburban Geese!   43
   Oops and Damns   43
   Shapes and Shadows   43

   Waiting to Dive   45
   Struggling With Sleeplessness in the Wilderness   45

The Eternal Instant	47
The Other Shoe	47
You Have This House	47
Similarities	49

Love After All Is

I Didn't Think	53
Phone Call	53
Balls of Yarn	55
Enveloping Silence	57
Love Is Given Freely	57
Escalator	59
The Book Shelf	61
Your Presence	63
You Are My Easel	63
When Driving at Night	65
My Redhead	67
Old to Young or Young to Old	69

You, Me, Us, We

The I in Thou	73
The One Missed	73
The Quilter	75

Returned	77
Sacred Places	77
Traveler—Boulder Terminal	79
Memories Big and Small	81
The Lonelies	83
Daisy Petals Along I-70 in Kansas at Night	85

Then There Are the Questions

Asheville, North Carolina	89
Bus Ride	91
Partings	93
Abstract Is Perfection	95
The Demise of the Blip on the Screen	97
Jews and Christians 2000	99
Real	101
Life Is a Line	103
The Korean War Memorial, September 1996	105
Jerusalem Donkey	107
Chapters	109
It's the Child Who Writes the Poems	111

Acknowledgments

For their encouragement and editing help, I thank the Galde Press crew: Phyllis Galde, my favorite publisher, for taking a chance on *Treading Water;* David Godwin, the executive editor, who puts everything in order and makes a book out of stuff; Angela Friesen for doing the copy editing and giving *Treading Water* rave reviews at the office; Andy Wood for his talented artwork; and Kathy Ritacco, who keeps everybody focused on getting Galde books out to the buying public.

Also, to friends and family, who graciously read some of my poems now and then, thank you for your helpful criticisms (really, I'm serious) and your kind encouragements.

Finally, to JoAnn, my wife, who just says, "Certainly you can write. Your stuff is good, so why procrastinate with worrying? Just do it." Thanks for being there when I needed that extra boost to get going.

Just People

Boy in the Oak

As I traveled the road of my journey, I saw him:

He rose from the deeply furrowed bark of the
      white oak—A boy child.
He was standing with arms spread backwards
      as if not quite free.
I first thought his legs were hidden by the tall
      grass at the base.
Then realized, from the knees down, he was
      still caught in the bark.

My mind rejected the image. I looked again.
He smiled, slipped from the oak and walked
      into the near by brush.
Turning where brush meets aspen growth,
      he grinned again.
I hesitated, stepped forward to follow—

He vanished through the aspen whispers.
The oak tree bore no evidence of imprinted bark.
The grasses stood unruffled, except by breezes.
Doubting my senses, I stepped back to the road.

Was he a woods elf?
                Creation's child?
                                A demon spirit?

                My soul mate?

Ahab, Ahab, Why Dost Thou?

Vengeance, Ahab, God says is His, not yours,
So then, why dost thou pursue this madness?

Are you the angry side of Job who questioned,
But in the end accepted the non-answer?

You Ahab, thrust your harpoon at the God of Mercy
    and demand an answer.

    What are we to learn from you, Ahab?

Carol

Over the years she has been the returning
    person,
Who swept into our world with smiles and stories
    of distant travels.
Like an autumn breeze that shifts the settled
    Leaves,
Her coming left us swirling, gently uplifted.

Sometimes, she came with gifts for birthdays,
    holidays and special occasions,
Gifts from enchanted places for us, the "stay at
    homes."
But always she brought the most precious gift—
    her presence.
She was compassionate with our losses and
    complimentary to our successes.

She carried the magical talent to enter each
    singular life within a group,
And gathered our stories into an album to hold
    as family when away.
She parted from us each time as she had come,
    leaving us gently stirred,
Waiting for the stimulating breeze to return from
    a distant somewhere.

Hester

Hester, when you walked through the burdock before the jail to stand the scaffold,
Women talked with scalding tongues, but one young heart spoke charity.
A dark heart in the outer ring hissed his vengeance.
Another pleaded to be released from guilt.

None knew then, your goodness would entwine them like the golden stitching of the A,
Nor could they fathom the surging emotion hidden in your heart beneath the shame.
And none could avoid the innocent beauty of the love child in your arms,
But you, Hester, know the secret of the Scarlet A as you stand the judges' allotted time.

Wear it proudly, Hester, for you have fooled them all.
The gossips blame the victim, they always do.
The bishop blames the devil, and Dimsdale cannot speak the truth.
The last, your doctor husband, will know the answer even to his own destruction.

Hester, bearing your secret, you will change
Adulterer to *Angel*, for you have known love.
A love that has opened hands to soothe the sick and empowered the eyes to penetrate evil.
Yes, Scarlet Woman, you know, and you have fooled them all with your silence.

She Is Eighty

She is 80—but a woman of passion.
"Yes," I said "and you still are."
She smiled—"In my heart it is so."

We sit at the table in her immaculate kitchen and talk of those things that
made up that space in the universe called her life.
She remembered to me the meanings she had given that passage,
And I listen with my heart's eyes.

When one listens with the eyes of the heart,
Words fade and meaning passes freely:
She was lovely as a girl.
She was vibrant in her womanhood.
She was praiseworthy in her motherhood.
She was fiery in her love of life.

Behind the age, thinned smile all of these remain,
as I listen with the eyes of my heart.

She

I was told she was in town again.
Some twenty-fifth reunion of some opening or other.
She chose not to call me…My friend said.
That's too bad…but really isn't.

There's no room for us to be together again.
No space between us would be wide enough to stem the years of wanting.
Too many people have come between.
Too many years of tending, to "the reasonableness of life"
The children, spouses, others and others, and still, others.

When we ended our time of intimacy, we understood,
Not only was the chapter to be closed, but the book never dared be open again.
How many times did I want to say, "Well, my friend what do you think about this?"
Or, "Tell me what you have learned about—Since."

How many times did I wonder if she remembered, as I did,
or thought about our then every day since.
How many times did I speak her name in the silence of my heart,
Never aloud for fear the walls would tumble, and the innocent would suffer?
Better the suffering of loss be carried by those who carry the joy of having had.

My heart aches that she chose not to call or seek me out.
My brain reasons the impossibility of breaching that span
which
we placed between us from fear.

My friend said, "She asked about you." Sort of like,
"How's he doing. How's his family."

Did her heart ache to know more?
Did she struggle with the temptation to say,
"I must see him before death separates us forever."
I did, when I saw the road sign to her town as I cruised by on the Interstate.

Well, in that distant then, we had talked about the binding of our souls,
About, how after the silent separation, they will be free to seek each other,
And how no one gets hurt…because isn't love eternal—and One?
At least that's what we believed, "once upon a time."

Isabella

Hurrah, Hurrah the baby came,
And Stacy and Paul are on to fame.
They're parents now, and that's a wow!
The biggest wow well worth a bow.

The kid's a girl with dark black hair,
And lashes that will bring a stare.
Cuz when she's grown and blinks her eyes,
Those fluttering lashes will mesmerize.

Men will flatter to gain her glance.
Parents will falter taking a stance,
Against her wishes and her wants,
As will Grandparents, uncles and aunts.

The world is different a new star has come,
The kid's a winner an obvious one.
She'll take this world and shake it gently,
And it will reward her most intently.

For as her namesake did in Spain
Isabella will extend a kindly reign,
To all good subjects gathered about
Willing to praise her with song and shout.

What Now, Frank?

It strikes me, Frank, that we have traveled
           seventy circlings about the sun.
There was a time we didn't pay much heed to
           those passings.
We didn't give the journey much thought,
           just traveled along for the ride.
We lived our stories as so many chapters in a
           novel without theme or plot.

But we have come to understand more deeply
           the value of moments.
We know that each sun rising is a miracle to
           savor until the next,
And we feel a need to make some sense of the
           journey,
To make all those circlings fit a larger story we
           call our life.

What now, Frank? What stories shall we tell?
Who shall we say we were as we traveled our
           stretch of infinity,
So that we can comprehend who we are at this
           moment,
Or rather, to decide who we want to be as now
           slips into tomorrow?

Puzzle Pieces

"How was the visit, Dad?"
My daughter asked talking to me on the phone.
She meant between Elmer and me.
We knew each other well as boys.

"Oh, we did some things.
You know, I showed him around the Cities,
And spent some time visiting with family,
But we mostly talked."

"You two reminiscing about your boyhood?"
My wife had asked the night of the second day.
"Yeah," I answered, but thought, *more than that.*
Mostly we had placed missing puzzle pieces.

Pieces of that puzzle we call *my life, his life,*
The pieces not placed before because of distance
        and time passing.
Pieces that had been left outside the border
        while living our separate lives,
In the fast lanes of family, work, getting ahead.

On the morning he was leaving,
There was an air of sadness in the parting,
We know the risks evident in the possibility of
        ever seeing each other again.
He with his survival from prostrate cancer; me
        from a triple bypass.

Something will finally come along some day,
And there won't be the randomness of survival.
But, there will remain connectedness.
Each of us will carry the puzzle pieces in our
      hearts labeled *Ed, Elmer.*

Piece Work

>See those summer shoes that college girl's
>wearing as she studies in the library?
>Piecework put those shoes on her feet

Someone killed the cow,
Someone skinned the cow,
Someone tanned the leather,
Someone cut the top and bottom leather for
       the straps.
Someone sewed the leather together to make
       the straps.
All done at so many pennies a piece

I once cut the leather that formed the straps, that wrapped the ankle of that college girl crossing one leg over the other and dangling her foot to catch the eye of him, whomever.

She's not aware that this cutter ignored a little imperfection on the leather so a certain pretty piecework sewer would have to leave her sewing machine and come bristling back to my machine.

"You stupid jerk. How can I make any money with you screwing up the leather," She said to me rather rudely.

"So you are a poor working girl," I said, "I'll take you to diner after shift." She stamps her foot, growls but smiles.

We walk together to the material rack to find the proper dyed leather and the other rack for a cutting mold that fits style and shoe

She scolds again.
I laugh.

My machine sits idle.
 (not making any money for the Company)
Her sewing machine?
 (a silent island in production's noisy river)

Piecework scam slammed. Boy meets girl.

The college boy smiles at co-ed diligently copying research material.
She dangles her legs with a little bounce to those summer shoes.

He closes the book on some professor's absolutely important assignment.
The co-ed blushes and with deliberate nonchalance uncrosses her legs.

"Nice shoes," he says." Break time for me. How about you? Coffee?"
"Why not," she says. "You broke my concentration anyway."

Another piecework scam slammed

Poker

"Hey, what's the game?"
"Follow the Whore again, just like the last deal.
You know, whatever card follows the Queen
        becomes wild."
Ah sevens are wild now, and I have one covered.
"I'll raise that. Play for twenty," *Sneaky me.*
Oops another Bitch showin' followed by a king.
"Kings are wild now, boys"
"Jeeze."
"Screw it I hate this game."

Another Queen followed by a three.
None in my hand. Well, I ought to drop. Aw—
"Call the bet."

"Pass the caramel corn will ya. You're hoggin' it all."
"Are you in this game or not?"
"Deal the cards! Deal the goddamned cards."
"Bet a quarter."
"You can if you want. But the rest of us will put in a
        dime. Not the last card."

Oops there's the last Queen.
"Damn!"
"Eights are now wild. Go ahead bet your quarter,"
"Where did you ever learn to deal? Check the bet."
And on goes the game. Has for years.

I've known these men most of my adult life:
Their wives, their kids, where they came from before here. None from here,
this town originally.

*What else, a little about their attitude toward their
jobs. We used to work together. All but two are
retired now.
What they do with time: Fish some, hunt some, travel
some, help out other people some.
Deal with the losses of aging. Pretty well I think.*

*Enough of us have been close to death in some
operating room.
We all put some kind of time serving God and
Country and using the GI bill afterwards.*

"Hey, will you deal the cards, dammit."
"You here to play cards or what? Jeeze."
"What's the game?'
"Depth Charge."
"Depth Charge? Will you get with the program?"
"Depth charge, dynamite they're all the same…"
"Dy-no mite!! Spell it out for ya, Jeeze"
 "Depth charge? God—"
"What's the game?"
"Man, open you're hearing aid. Dyn-no–mite!"
"I hate that game."
"Hey, what's the matter? You're havin' fun, right?"
"Dealer! You forgot to anti…"
"Put 'er in. Fifty cents and no Canadians"
"Watch 'im."

*The cards fly with the ease of thousands of shuffles
and deals.
So at the end of the night, you know, we'll meet on
the sixteenth of next month.
Hopefully we'll all be alive, none too sick to play, all
of our kids, wives, grandkids well.*

Boring?
No—Death is boring, long and boring.
Life is doing simple stuff.
What the hell, we're havin' fun aren't we?

Julian of Norwich

Julian, God said to you,
"All that is, is no larger than that hazelnut."
"But I will keep it holy," He assured you.
You held it in your hand and wondered,
"It is so tiny, so insignificant?"
But, Julian, God said, "That is all there is."

Whatever is created comes from His love.
He shall not allow it to fall into the abyss of nothingness.
He loves what he has created; He maintains its existence.
And all that "is" shall remain well in His eyes.

Mary

August 31, 2002 – Dear Mary

Mary how come they call you a virgin?
I used to believe the story of a spirit, not a man, entering your body,
But now at seventy I wonder why God would create a process of love,
And then deny it in the birth of His anointed one.

No Mary, I suspect they who presented you as a virgin in their books,
Found love too powerful a force to tame within themselves,
So they denied its existence in the woman's body that housed God.
They named, as shameful, the Creator's gift to caring lovers.

Mary, I suspect that in the wondrous springtime of early womanhood,
You shared your passions in abandonment as God intended,
And shuddering to the flooding wash of sensuality,
Released your body to respond to the spirit of new creation.

A Prayer to Lady Wisdom

SOPHIA,
You are with the Father always from the beginning.

Where do You hide now,
        while the children of His world squabble?
Those who claim Him for their own,
        detest all others who accept Him differently.

SOPHIA
Your knowledge of God is a Oneness as is no other.

Lead us wayfarers
        from our self-induced darkness;
Take us away from gray doubt,
        to brilliant clarity of understanding.

SOPHIA,
You shared His love and nurtured His created beings.

Come again touch our essence with
        Your understanding.
Bring us to knowing Your peace
        as He wills it to be.

***** In the Book of Wisdom ***She*** rescued, protected, saved, guided and delivered. These are actions normally accorded to God, or to one who is an intimate of the Creator. Who then is Wisdom? Where is She now? In which of the great patriarchies has she been enveloped?

The Good Man
At Least Some Folks Say He's Good

This guy they say is good,
        Just guess what he says about forgiving,
He says
        "Forgive seven times seventy."
Really, that's his answer, and you know
        that old mystical number seven thing?
Something to do with infinity,
        like infinity times infinity equals infinity.

Then he adds, "Forgive those who hurt you,"
        Now how smart is that in this world?
What would happen to wars
        with that kind of forgiving?
Think about that for a while.
We'd have to turn weapons into plowshares or
        something.
And, who'd buy plowshares, a few farmers maybe?

And, guess what?
He's got this other thing, this neighbor idea.
Go ahead ask him, "Who is my Neighbor?"
You know what his answer is? Really is? "Everybody!"
Everybody? Yeah right, and especially your enemies,
        him, her all of them.

Well, those are the ideas this good man has—
Good or not, He's got to be a little crazy.

Bits and Pieces Lightly Played

Sun Dress

You stood there naked under your summer dress,
I hesitated to seek further than a tender touch to your cheek.

You were like an unopened book as you stood quietly waiting
With the sunlight shaping shadowy enticements
            under the thin material,

But I knew, once those mysterious shapes blotting out the
           sun's rays became skin and flesh,
    My soul would fly beyond return.

Cherry Blossom

Cherry blossom, exquisite
Bursts into existence;
Lingers just this moment;
Departs in faded death.

Love, boundless joy discovered,
Entwines with passionate fury;
Grips the heart too briefly;
Passes with our passing.

Life, beautiful gift, unearned;
Swells us into being;
Releases without warning;
Gone before its time.

Ifs and Hopes

If all our hopes were *come to bes,* instead of
what ifs;
They would have turned to *certainties* instead of
should have beens.

Kissed Me

Easy kissed me in the park.
Like a thief he stole that kiss,
Among fall colors bright and dark,
From one slightly perplexed miss.

No one's kissed me quite like that,
But Easy did, and I am glad.
There he stands with that impish grin,
Now I wonder, "Was I had?"

Little Boys and Little Girls

Little boys are made of :
chromosomes, genes and testosterone potential.

Little girls are made of the same
chromos and genos, but they have estrogen to come.

Someday, together
they will become the stuff and nonsense of love—

Now isn't that a scary thought?

Oh! Those Suburban Geese!

What are the geese saying in honking laughter as they fly their Vs overhead?
What secret do they know waddling about fouling our lawns and ponds?
Why don't they leave earlier for those more inviting southern climes?
What's the big joke that they seem to share under our protection?

Of course, we have done our share to foul our own waters,
So the surfaces don't freeze like they used to—
Maybe those geese hanging around are
Laughing with scorn,
That we don't understand
our own shortsighted foolishness.
Naw, they're not that smart—are they?

Oops and Damns

Creation takes practice—
I'm sure even God
Had his, "oops and damns"
We call it *"evolution."*

Shapes and Shadows

I know the shape so well and yet,
I do not wish to disturb the shadows,
For as they lengthen in the evening dusk,
My soul too stretches beyond the bounds and limits of my life.

Waiting to Dive

The blue ocean sends its signals in
                              sprinkled splatters
                                    of sun
      specks.
The call grows
      in my motion
            intoxicated mind—

                "Come Home."

Come home? What the hell—Home?

      A blue ocean
           creased by white
    tipped waves?
    A salty taste
           through tongue and nose?

                Home?

Struggling With Sleeplessness in the Wilderness
(1976)

Sink summit somewhere beneath,
The sounds of somber, soddened songsters,
And softly salute the soundless sands of sleep.

Then

Perhaps propitious prose will point to paths profound.

The Eternal Instant

A planet cools,
Gaseous dioxide dissipates,
Oxygen permeates amoebic responses,
Paramecium
      to lizards
           to apes
                to man
                      to choice.

The Other Shoe

I sat on the edge of the bed this morning –
Pulled on one pant leg;
Stood –
Stepped into the other leg,
And pulled those *cotton pickers* up!

"The other shoe didn't fall last night," I said,
"And that's just fine with me;
"It's gonna be another grand day—just grand!"

You Have This House

You have this house with many rooms
Filled with furniture.
Then for a while filled with children and furniture.
Now you have this house with many room
Filled with furniture—and so.

Similarities

As lightning prefaces thunder,
And the rumbles shake the earth,
Your entrance into a room full of people
Shatters the murmuring chatter into silence.

Love After All Is

I Didn't Think

I didn't think this would have happened so
soon,
That I became quickly caught
Between the dominance of my sun,
And the waxing, waning, mystery of your moon.

Does God plan these ironies,
Or do lovers choose the impossible themselves,
To prove that some unwritten code of the heart,
Transcends all laws of celestial movement?

Phone Call

I answered. You spoke simple words,
"Hello, I just thought I'd let you know—"
There was no need for you to finish. I knew the rest,
And I felt that knot of loneliness inside me stretch, then untie.

I smiled and sighed a contented breath.
"I feel the same," I said.
You chuckled softly—the magic!
Yes, the magic of loving and being loved.

Love chooses love without reason only choice.
Lovers sort through words attempting to find meaning,
But, eventually, they can only sigh or chuckle and agree.
They are enveloped within the mystical vapors rising from
Love's Wine.

Balls of Yarn

She was sitting in the gliding rocker reading.
I sat in the other sipping my coffee and watching her.
She wasn't aware of my gaze; too intent on Harry Potter.
Of all things, Harry Potter!

Well, that's her, keeping up with the grandkids, I suppose.
Anyway, I wondered as I watched her,
As balls of yarn go, are each of us gathering or unraveling?
The ball that is her, the ball that is me are they growing or shrinking?

But as a couple, are those strands more entwined or less?
Compared to what? To a time of not knowing each other or when the kids were small?
How do we answer that question since we are never the same people we were before?
Yesterday, ten years ago, forty years ago? Who were we?
Who are we now?

Looking up from her book she met my gaze.
"You're staring," she said and asked off-handedly, "What are you thinking now?"
"Oh nothing." I answered "Just drifting sort of, relaxing my brain."
She smiled somehow knowing I'm not telling what is really going on "in there."

"You need to read this next," she said and slipped back into the world of dragons and witches.
That's an unusual book for her to be reading, I thought.
This grandmother thing has really changed the color in the strands of her yarn.
I sighed a half laugh. She gave me a momentary "What now?" glance and returned to reading.

So that's it, I thought. *Although each of us expands the circumference of our gathered yarn,*
There are knots along the way which serve as markers of permanent "who you are".
She knows them as well as I do, for it is at those points our yarns entangle.
As one pulls on a surface strand, it gathers as a fixed point of us in the other.

She closes the book on Harry and looks toward me; gives a slight shake of her head.
"I suppose one of us ought to make lunch," she says knowing which knot she's tugging.
"I will." I announce. "You're reading. Besides must be my turn to tighten an old knot."
She frowns. *Where has he taken his brain this time?* She wonders and opens her book.

I get up, roll into the kitchen and wrap a strand around the handle of the Frig.
The fixings are there, cold cuts in the bin, Mayo on the shelf, bread in the freezer.
Glancing back through the door, I realize, *She's done it again tugged an old knot.*
She's reading; I'm making lunch. Roll reversal of the yarn balls. They just keep expanding.

Enveloping Silence

When I am with you in silence, we are most joined as one.
Enveloped by the silence and each other.
We are as the fish is in water,
And the hawk in air.

The fish needs water to be a fish,
The water—the fish to present its liquidity.
Can the hawk soar without air's wafting currents?
If the hawk were not present, would we know the mystery of air?

In the completeness of silence, there is only unity between us.
If we disturb the silence by speaking our separateness,
We flounder on the beach or fall through a void.
And—There is only emptiness within nothing.

Love Is Given Freely

You have shared the being that is you with me.
You have set no limits to the gifts.
You have opened your heart of hearts to me.
You have pressed your inner life's warmth about me.

And,
Because of these gifts, I have given others more attention and more of my love.

And
Because of your giving, I have found a closer connection with the Creator.

But mostly
I have tried to return the love you have given me.

Escalator

Our eyes met across the chasm separating the up and down escalator.
We held each other almost instantly as we began our rise and descent.
The smiles trickled across the maps we call our faces.

We did not reach out as we passed in the close mid-point.
The brows were still wrinkled question marks,
But the eyes never faltered.

Words wanted to form the wide, open expression of "Yes!"
Yes?—Yes what?
The Yes of, "I would but—"

We broke contact only to be sure of our step off to solid floor.
When we turned, I now at the top; you at the bottom,
We did not say but heard, "I'm sorry. The ride has ended too soon."

But it hasn't, really.
You move across from me on every escalator I ride.
I have not forgotten, "The Yes."

"Nor I."

The Book Shelf

So where do we file it, this love of ours, on the
    bookshelf of life?
Does it have a place between some categories of
    other books like,
Moments to be Remembered or *Times Together Best
    Forgotten?*
Well, maybe those are too broad; I think we need
    specific classifications.

Like: *Angels We Debated:* You know, the one
    topping the Christmas tree,
That you liked 45 years ago much to my chagrin, but
    now I insist it be there.
Or *Tough Decisions Made:* "Which one you want
    before the sitter comes:
The oldest vomiting in the bathroom, or youngest
    diarrehing in the crib?"

Then there's *Paying Bills Or Not?* Remember, at the
    end of the month,
Dumping the bills on the kitchen table and playing
    the yellow Daisy Game.
Pulling them from the pile one by one, like white
    petals from the flower,
"These charge interest; these don't; this one does this
    one doesn't."

But those were the later years.
At least later than when we were young lovers
    without kids.
We could have *Kisses Taken; Given?* The first time I
    kissed you, remember?

You weren't even sure you liked me, you said, but
    you kissed me back.

You always defended, "It was just a natural response.
    What did I expect a girl to do?"
Well, I certainly didn't think you'd do nothing back!
Anyway, what you did do left me with all kinds of
    expectations, so—
Natural Responses, a very thick book, must fit
    somewhere, don't you think?

Of course you fibbed back then so many books ago,
    You really liked me, didn't you?
Anyway, you kept responding, naturally.—
I mean, children and grandchildren aren't just
    miracles—or are they?
If nothing else, they've filled a lot of our bookshelves
    in these after years.

Your Presence

When the poets speak of love,
They talk of you as surgeons:
Your eyes your teeth, your unmentionables, but—
I have come to know the wonder of your presence.

You are not here now.
You are elsewhere placing your being among others,
Enveloping them with a mystical aura, which wraps
      my heart in softness when I am with you.

What of eyes and breast and cascading hair?
Those come into being from the distant before
birth,
And fade into the unknowable after death,
But your being has entered into mine for all eternity.

Though I long for the fit of our *whos*
In the absence of *alabaster arms* and *rose petal lips,*
I am aware of something other than me entangled
      within the web of my soul.

      For I am loved!

You Are My Easel

You are the easel, on which I rest my canvas,
And the palette from which I paint life's meaning.
The colors flow from you and spread their beauty
      into landscapes.

There is purple in the clouds and in the shadows of snow banks,
And late evening swells with pastels that soften life's sharp edges.
Because you are, night's lonely darkness is a mere restful reprise,
Prefacing morning's rose-tinted sea, jeweled with twinkling diamonds.

When Driving at Night

At night on the road to somewhere, anywhere,
    I think about you.
As oncoming headlights approach and pass into darkness,
My mind wanders, then recalls—the kisses.

Where did our lips first touch so briefly,
That we were not sure if they had touched at all?
But now as I stare into the night ahead,
My heart swells to near bursting with the memory.

Another kiss came later,
Not with such unexpectedness this time.
We looked a long time into eyes that questioned,
Eyes that invited—eyes that smiled, "Yes."

Then there were the others.
Those we clung to with parted lips until—Breath!
Followed by laughter and glistening eyes,
And an understanding we had joyfully exchanged our worlds.

I'm smiling because little did we know those kisses,
Would seek other places little kissed—never kissed.
Or did we?
Somehow did we understand from that first delight,
There was no returning.
    There were no more surprises.
        There were only little gasps of wonder.

It doesn't matter all that much, the motives pure or otherwise.
The truth remains:
As long as our hearts beat within the cavities of our bodies,
        and the secret places our emotions,
Memories of that first kiss and all that followed come back at
        night when our spirits wander.

My Redhead

She was a redhead. I've always admired redheads.
They remind me of Gwenivere of Camelot.
Anyway, in the Lancelot role I play in my mind,
My Gwen is a redhead and she comes from Scottish stock.
Is that in Arthur's story? Nope. I made it up.
But then again, Why not? It's all as we tell ourselves, anyway—Isn't it?

You see, the attendants, the family they don't know about Gwen and me,
Or about our land at the foot of the highlands by the sea.
They think my brain cells are twisted, lost chords, but they are really
                entwined lovers' knots.

I laugh at the visitor who whispered, "Too Bad. He had such a wonderful
   mind."
But they don't know about her, my red head—
Who actually came from a barstool in Tampa when I was on that three
   day pass.
For one weekend she was Gwenivere, and I, Lance
              as we made love on the cool, night beaches.

When they shake their heads in anguish and sigh, "Alzheimer's my god!"
They do not know of you, Red from the Sea Breeze Lounge,

Nor how you tossed your hair back over your shoulder sitting across the
   booth
              from me at breakfast.
Nor how those few strands played with your ear as you turned to speak
   with
              the waitress.
Nor how those same strands cascaded down covering my face when you
   kissed me, as I lay pinned between your straddling knees.

Nor do they understand how we rode the black charger on the hard sand along
>   the Scottish coast, and I was lost in the flaming tresses of your love.

Oh Shakespeare, you were so right, "What fools these mortals be."
They prefer to dawdle in the real world of things and shoulds and should nots,
But not me! I've settled in being Lance with Gwen in my *New World* of—
>   misplaced, modified memories.

Old to Young
Or Young to Old

"Love? Huh. Old man, what can you tell me of love?
I who am at the height of my energy, I sustain.
You, who needs assists from the pharmacy,
What can you tell me?"

"I can tell you nothing
Because you must learn for yourself,
Or not learn at all.
That is your choice."

"What you must learn or not is this:
Love's energy expands itself within that
Which is neither sustainable through the pharmacy,
Nor fed from some gland of excitability."

You, Me, Us, We

The I in Thou
(Apologies to Martin Buber)

My I-thou is you.
We are connected by a bridge no longer than a heartstring.
Without becoming something other than each self,
We are as near to one as two can be.

There is no other bridge through which we are as one,
Except the One to whom we all were thous,
And who remains with each of us as Self until—
Each thou returns to ever be as one with I in All.

The One Missed

I have so much to say to her.
I miss the times of sharing and growing together.
I learn something and think, *I'll tell her of it.*—
When? Death has spoken the final word.

There are to be no further conversation between us.
Our quiet exchanges have passed with her passing.
But I am not alone in this silence of her absence,
For I am bound to the memory of her uniqueness.

The Quilter

When you gather her quilt about your shoulders,
Or tuck its softness under your child,
Or stroke satin edging while you suck your thumb,
Or hold a loved one beneath its warmth——
Touch the stitches and—Remember the Quilter.

She sewed love with each careful push of the needle.
Sometimes to the accompaniment of relaxing music,
Sometimes while she considered the issues discussed
on MPR,
And, often as she stitched in special prayers for the
intended one,
So, touch the stitches and remember the Quilter.

Each piece of cloth and every color was chosen by
her for you.
Each turn of the quilting form brought her closer to
you.
Each needle prick or aching wrist was shrugged away
with thoughts of you.
So, each night as you snuggle under soft, comforting
warmth,
Remember the Quilter and her Quilts.

There are as many quilts as there are marriages + 1
and 13 grandchildren,
And still others given as gifts to family, neighbors
and friends.
Others too were made for strangers battered by life
and desperately wanting.
So as you wonder at the count so many, remember
her, the Quilter.

In the morning when you carefully arrange your quilt
on the bed,
Remember, and send prayers for happiness to—

THE QUILTER

Returned

You will be home today, so I am at peace. I am settled.
The absence was short, the hours, however, were long.
They needed to be filled with *doings* and *avoidings*,
Especially when I went to where you usually are but weren't.

I am pleased with your return, and I am whole.

Sacred Places

There are places that become Sacred, because you were there with me.
They can be as sublime as a walking path near some lake,
Or as common as a grocery store isle in which we have lost each other,
Then after some hectic annoyance, see the familiar waiting to be found.

Our sacred places are not those houses of prayer,
Although some are, the mosque-cathedral in Spain,
Or the folding chair, gym church in Minneapolis,
Or melding into the moment of some young people's wedding.

But Sacredness comes not from the place,
It permeates those being in a state of grace with another other.
That other may be God, or you, or some another.
Does it matter for the being that links in grace with the Sacred?

There is no great mystery in our sacred places.
They are entered into with love,
And where there is love, there is "grace."
For—there cannot be separateness in that moment.

Traveler—Boulder Terminal

I sit waiting in the terminal, and they pass;
The bodies, the faces, the physical impressions.
I long for you among them,
Although I know you are not to be present.

But as I wait and watch,

A mother passes holding hands with two children;
you are there.
A traveler closes his book, rises and leaves my sight.
Within his momentary passing,
you are there.
Running children on the moving walkway
exhibit your energy;
A crying child stamping her feet your frustrations.

There is no loneliness as that of being alone among
others in private aliveness.
They breathe the same air, share the same light,
spend their allotted time as I do.
Yet, they and I remain detached and apart as we
traverse life's web together.

But you and I?
Between us, there is no separation even as we are
separated.

Memories Big and Small

Who are these people in my living room?
They have the same names we gave our kids,
But these bodies are big, really big!
Couldn't get them all in the station wagon, even the
                              nine passenger.
Couldn't gather them into the tent on a rainy camping
                              night, either.
They'd never fit sprawled out among the piled up
                              sleeping bags.
Beside they'd be debating the meaning of the story
                              I was reading,
Arguing some weird political or religious view in
            "Little Train That Could."

They used to play games in the basement, and I
                              worried about them falling.
The floor down there was hard concrete, the walls
                              were cement block.
Somehow when they bounced against the wall or
                              flopped on the floor,
They always got up laughing, giggling, screaming
                              with joyous excitement.

But here in the living room, they don't move that
                              much. They talk.
They tell about the games they encounter in the big
                              people's world.
Games with other walls to bounce off and hard floors
                              to flop down on,
But they still know how to laugh or giggle or scream
                              as they get up.

Well, their conversation has shifted to stories from those camping trips.
"Remember when dad—when mom—at the—in the nine passenger?"
"The time when—I was pushed—Right! Making your own reality again."
"We all remember. You fell off that rock.—Well, I was just a little kid."

"Hey grandpa," one of their small people interrupts, "Did my mom jump or fall in the lake?
"Well—I think she flew. She was such a charming, little angel—Just like you."

Reality? Whose?
They each have their own, and I have mine
But—We all were there.
That's the reality. That's the memory.

The Lonelies

I'm lying here, still and quiet.

Quieter even, than when quiet was what I had to be as a kid.
Like in church when I couldn't see over those high backed pews,
Or at suppertime when visitors were talking or grace was being said,
Or at Uncle John's funeral when he was so old, and I
didn't even know him. "Anyway," adults said, "He had had a good life,
and we all go sometime."

Later there were the demanded school silences of
adolescence.
Like in Spanish 12 when the language tape was
playing,
And all good students (of course it was an AP class)
had to listen!
Even though Sally Shavino was sitting in the seat
next to me,
And I wanted to talk to her. (Actually, I did once.
Much to her chagrin.)

Now, all grown up, I'm here quieter and silenter, than
all those other times.
I don't like these Lonelies. When the ache comes it
hurts my heart too much.
I want to talk with you, even more than I ever wanted
to bother that Sally.
But you? You're gone. You have chosen not to be
with me. Why?
Is this a "for good"? Are you playing some game I
don't know the rules to?

What ever happened to always?

Daisy Petals Along I-70 in Kansas at Night

We were driving through Kansas at night:

Following our own headlights through a tunnel of darkness.
With everything on the peripheral in blackness
        except some signs, places to eat, gas to get.

And the marker posts:
Those that look like farm fence posts painted white on top.
The ones I never have stopped to learn how far apart they are.
They flit past faster than you can count when you're a kid.

You were asleep in the passenger's seat,
And I was still fuming from one of those disagreeable
misunderstandings couples have on the road.
Something important like—
    When shall we stop to eat?
    Which route is better?
    And I wish you hadn't said that
        just when we were leaving their house.

Anyway, I glanced at you and wondered,
    After all these years does she still?
And the old daisy petal game jumped into my mind,
    She loves me. She loves me not.

The white tipped marker posts became
    the petals tossed aside to the alternating questions.
The tire noise snapping across the expansion cracks clicked—
    "She loves me? She loves me not—She loves me?

Yes, she does, no she doesn't—she does – she—"
And then the bridges loomed black doubts with each passing.
(Kansas is full of overhead bridges) They whispered,
    "Maybe she doesn't.
        Maybe you've grown apart and are only
            held together by habit, by kids?"

You shifted in the seat and opened your eyes.
"Where are we?" you asked.
"Somewhere in Kansas," I answered.
"We've been in Kansas a long time. It's a big state.
    You must be tired. Want me to drive?"
"Yeah, thanks," I said and smiled quiet joy.
    "The next rest stop's coming up soon."
"OK. Wake me then," you said, and snuggled into the pillow
    wedged against the door and seat.

I looked into the tunnel of light and grinned.
The white tips flitted a new routine of accompaniment to
    the clacking concrete.
        "Yes she does!
            Yes she does.
                You bet she does."

I laughed at the dark, gloomy bridge passing overhead.
    "Don't sweat the small stuff—She does."

Then There Are the Questions

Asheville, North Carolina

As we walked down the street in Asheville,
Frank approached the guy of the young couple sitting
outside the noisy bar.
"You from here?" he asked. "Do you know where we
can find the Y?"
"No," the young man answered.
His girl companion was in a cell phone. She wasn't
from here either.

Frank asked the question several times at other
outside tables.
Those people weren't from here either.
I asked, "You think anyone's from here, Frank?"
"Doesn't seem that way," he said, then added,
"And if they do answer 'yes' don't bother asking
about ordinary places.
Forget about finding the museum, the zoo or the post
office.
Since they live here, they won't know."

"Oh," I said, but wondered to myself,
*Are any one of us really from here whether we are or
not?*

Bus Ride

So God –
If You are in everything,
You must be within me,
And if You are, am I You too?
Or must I return to You that which is You in me?

Well, if that's the plan, I do know the destination.
I've been with You before people discovered time.
Now I continually study maps and ponder different
        routes over the territory trying to return.
However, the roads lead into each other, and it all
        seems rather confusing.

Supposedly, some declare, they know a bus that
        runs on the right freeway.
All a person need do is buy a ticket from the proper
        people to get a seat.
Unfortunately, their time and departure schedules are
        many and blurred;
And the ticket sellers change hats so often one can't
        take them very seriously.

So God –
If You are in everything,
You must be within me,
And if You are, You might consider a slight hint.
Maybe a holy whisper from the mountain top, or
        directions in the sand.

Partings

Harry Horn was here this past weekend.
We talked of our school, of course,
Of times we had known as kids,
And of classmates we knew and know.

What does it matter all these memories, all this talk?
When he and Fran leave and head for Alaska,
Why do I feel sad and want more, not only of them,
But of the others, especially the dead?

Is it aging? Being 65?
Knowing that many threads have been broken,
And many more will be severed until mine to all
        others will unravel and break.
Or is there something else? After all, Julian says
        "All is well and will be well as it should be."

    Even these partings are they as "all should be"?
One would think there are only as many leavings as
        there are joinings,
But that doesn't seem so; the *good byes* stick deeper,
And stay longer but are loaded with hope.

Hope for the next time, the taking in a hug and
        holding with arms and with heart.
Ah, but regret comes with death; some we didn't hold
        long enough or deep enough back then.
Could we, can we ever hold long enough or hard
        enough before having to leave or let go?

Harry's motor home has turned the corner at Main.
Their stay was pleasant despite the rain.
We talked of our work, our kids, our friends in
    common, our very fortunate lives.
Despite the pains of loss and illness and deep-seated
    good byes, we are here among life.

Abstract Is Perfection

The abstract is perfection
A circle is nothing more than itself.
A triangle cannot be confused with a square.
A hexagon has six perfect sides.

These are what they are.
They are perfection.
But where are they?
If we see them they would not be.

If Perfection is as perfection is and nothing else.
If God is perfection as are the geometric forms,
Then God cannot be more than God is,
And all that God created is as God created.

Nothing then, is more or less than it is.
And everything is as God intended,
So what is there to change?
I wonder.

The Demise of the Blip on the Screen

When the end comes in the night,
Does it not bang but whimper,
Or is it even quieter than that?

Think about it,
    That silence of the Blip
        Disappearing from the
            Computer screen?

Think of all the computerized lists deleting the name:
When the heart stops, and the mind leaves the brain,
    And the spirit returns to the henceforth.

        the magazine distributors
        the charity causes
        the catalogue companies
        and, of course,
        the credit card distributors
        the bank records
        They all go blip, blip, blip

Then eventually even:
Military records
Church Directory
Social security
All go blip, blip, bl-i-p

    And then, the screen goes green empty.

Jews and Christians 2000

When you tear away all the trappings,
The Torah, The Scrolls,
The Cross, the Crib,
Where do they differ?

The stories—
The stories they tell themselves,
The stories they believe in,
Their truths as they know them to be.

After all is said and done,
Even the Ten Commandments,
And the Sermon on the Mount,
What keeps them apart?

Their basic stories,
One, the Sinaitic Covenant with a People.
The other a promise to each person,
That peace comes with the Birthing Resurrection.

The Messiah they talk of,
Will come, has come, is coming, came and went.
They're not even talking of the same Messiah,
Unless they talk of the First and Second as The One.

Then what? They must re-create the stories,
A new twist, a new covenant, a new sermon.
The Net! The Net knows all, tells all, gives all.
One need only access the Internet, and

        SHE will respond.

Real

Tell me my friend, which is real,
As I sit gently rocking remembering us then?
The memory of our youthful world,
Or this old man slowly moving back and forth?

If real is the moment of experience,
And my emotions swell within me,
As tears of remembrance flood my eyes,
Where truly is my being?

Is the resting body only an empty shell,
That decomposes into the passing moments of time?
And the feelings so intense the reality we will take—
Wherever we go from here?

           If we take anything at all?

Life Is a Line

Life is a line or is a circle.
The beginning comes from nowhere
The end goes to nowhere;
Or the beginning is the end and the end the beginning.
The beginning is a change from nothing.
The end is a change to always.
Or neither is either.
Life is a line or is a circle.

The beginning starts at this point; the end finishes at this point,
Or the points are one and the same.
The beginning announces me.
The end hides me.
Or they blend into instantaneous forever and never in noisy silence.

The beginning the end; the end the beginning
Are they?
Or is the question without answer and the instant eternity.

The Korean War Memorial September 1996

I went to the Korean War Memorial today.
Out of curiosity, I think.
Curiosity to see if I would be touched in some way.

Not that I served in Korea,
But because I could have served and not come back
Or come back all shot up,
Or…all messed up from shooting others.

That Bronze patrol forever walking up the hill
With M1's, carbines, a light machine gun and a radio.
They're all wearing ponchos.
And oddly—
It is raining, a slight, chilly drizzle here in
Washington, D.C., this September day.

I could have been one of them and wasn't.
I was twenty or so then. Did my time in places where
there wasn't any enemy.
Yet, I'm sad: 54,000 Americans, and, allies—
hundreds of thousands. Enemies? Even more.

I wonder sometimes:
If we piled all the dead from all of Mankind's wars,
would the pile touch Heaven?
And, what would God say?

Jerusalem Donkey

I was just a dumb donkey hanging around the square.
Then some guys came and dragged me from my tie
                              up and feed.
They put this skinny guy on my back
                              (He was heavy anyway.)
I thought,
Who the hell are these guys to come around and ruin
                              my Sunday?

Well, these guys pulled us to the Jerusalem road,
                              and hey!
Both sides were jammed with people
                              shoutin' and singin' "Hosannas."
I felt really like I was some big time Perchon
                              in a parade.
I straightened up and strode forward, like I hadn't
                              since I was a colt.

Some little kid, excited with all the commotion,
                              waved and said,
"Daddy look at that horse the man is riding. Isn't he a
                              nice color gray?'
"He's not a horse son, "the father answered in his
                              adult authority
"He's just some dumb donkey trying to be a horse."

Well at that, I whinnied like a bolting racehorse, and
                              jerked forward.
The man sitting on top leaned to my ear and gently
                              whispered,
"Settled down old friend, and we will get through
                              this together."
I did and pranced down the rode in proud style.

Now, the people waving palm branches tossed them
                              on the road.
Those soft leaves felt great. My old feet were hurtin'
                        from the cobblestones.
"Soon," my rider said, "We will need to have
patience. They will shout other words. They want
more than I can give. Seems like they always do."

"Well, you can count on me,' I said.
But not being sure why his voice was so sad,
And why the crowds had become silent, I added,
"I'm just a dumb donkey, but you seem a well
intentioned guy, so—."

Then the rocks replaced the branches, and the jeers
the Hosannas.

Chapters

It's like the chapters are closing.

One of parents, others of brothers, sisters,
        this friend or that one, or neighbors.
The past loving when we raised so much passion
        just at the touch of our lips.
Our near lifetime of marriage:
        with memories of places, vacations, jobs.
The children running in the basement:
        now grownups sitting in the living room?
The ideas and ideals,
        the pride in country, the belief in God?
The last, final chapter,
        the cancer, the heart failure, the accident.
Is it "Hello, God" or "Good-bye, God."
        with the close of the back cover?

It's The Child Who Writes the Poems

"It is the child in you that writes the poems," he said
with some disdain.
My friend that is, he told me that the other day.
"Adults don't spend time spinning useless feeling
stuff," he said.
"Grownups deal with the real world, that which really
counts,
Commerce, production, wars, stuff like that."
"Wow! I didn't know," I said. "How silly of me!"

To order additional copies of this book,
please send full amount plus $4.00 for
postage and handling for the first book and
50¢ for each additional book.

Send orders to:

Galde Press, Inc.
PO Box 460
Lakeville, Minnesota 55044-0460

Credit card orders call 1–800–777–3454
Phone (952) 891–5991 • Fax (952) 891–6091
Visit our website at www.galdepress.com

Write for our free catalog.